A Slug Is Born

Written by Brylee Gibson

Look under the log.
Look at all the eggs.
Slugs are in the eggs.

2

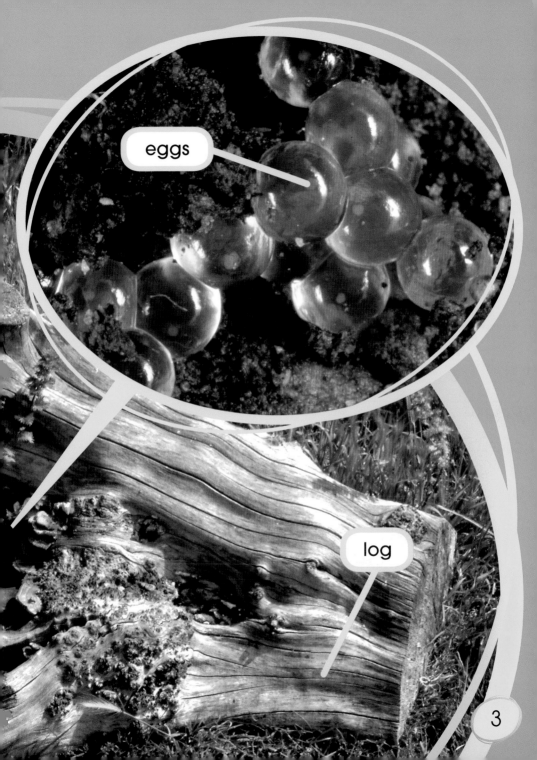

eggs

log

3

The eggs are like jelly.
You can see into the eggs.
You can see the slug.

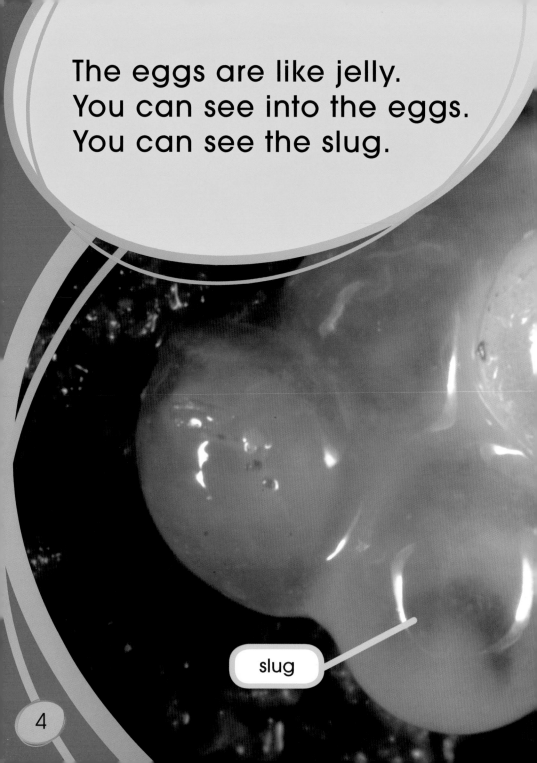

slug

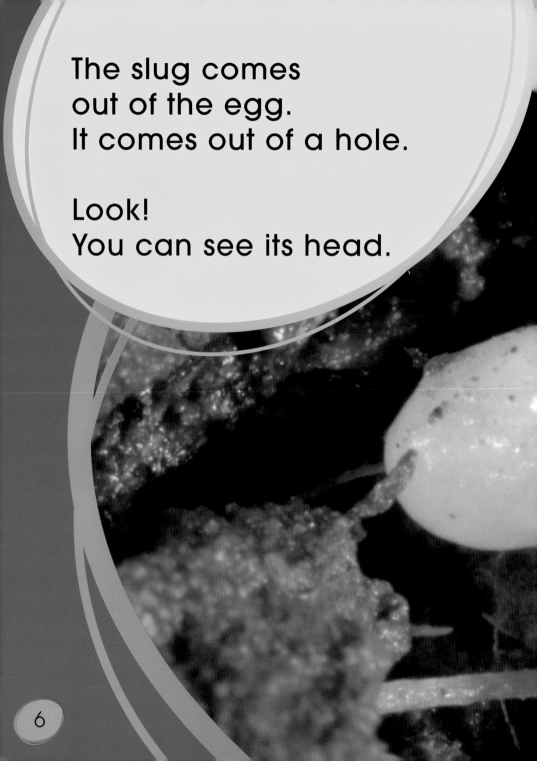

The slug comes
out of the egg.
It comes out of a hole.

Look!
You can see its head.

head

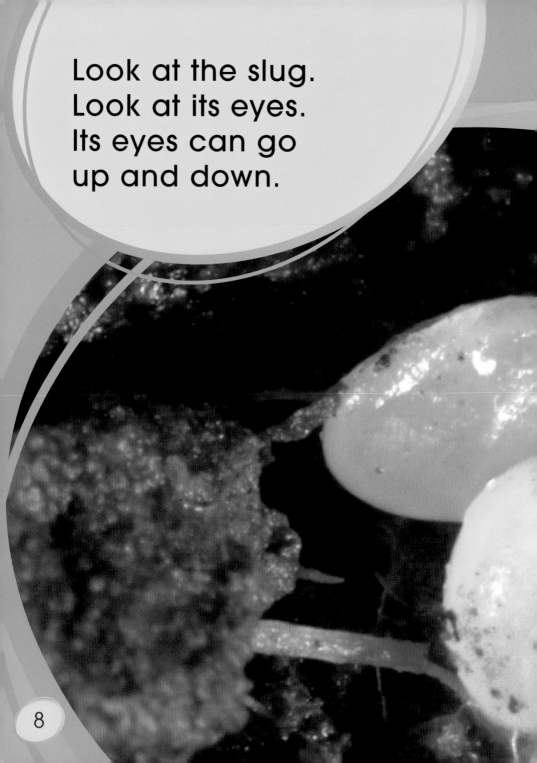

Look at the slug.
Look at its eyes.
Its eyes can go
up and down.

eyes

The slug is
out of the egg.
It will go away.

The egg will stay
under the log.

egg

slug

Look at all the slime.
The slime will
help the slug go
over the ground.

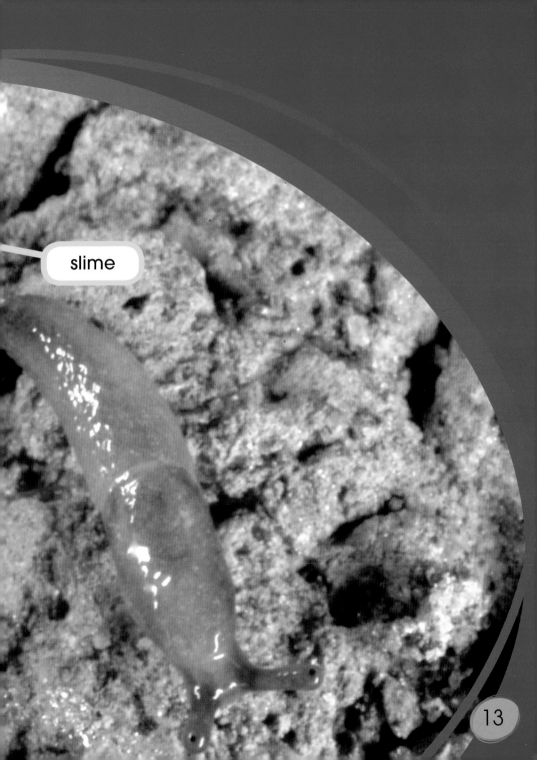

slime

13

The slug looks for
food to eat.
It can eat leaves.
Look at all the holes.

hole

Index

leaf

Guide Notes

Title: A Slug Is Born

Stage: Early (2) – Yellow

Genre: Nonfiction

Approach: Guided Reading

Processes: Thinking Critically, Exploring Language, Processing Information

Written and Visual Focus: Photographs (static images), Index, Labels

Word Count: 114

THINKING CRITICALLY
(sample questions)

- Look at the title and read it to the children. Ask the children what they think this book might be about.
- Focus the children's attention on the index. Ask: "What are you going to find out about in this book?"
- If you want to find out about food that slugs can eat, which page would you look on?
- If you want to find out about slugs' eyes, which page would you look on?
- What do you think might happen to the egg that stays under the log?
- How do you think the slime helps the slug move over the ground?

EXPLORING LANGUAGE

Terminology
Title, cover, photographs, author, photographers

Vocabulary
Interest words: slug, eggs, log, jelly, hole, head, eggs
High-frequency words: all, its, stay, looks
Positional words: in, into, out, up, down, under, over

Print Conventions
Capital letter for sentence beginnings, periods, exclamation mark